Flowers and How They Grow

Carrie Stuart

Science

Rosen Classroom Books & Materials™
New York

There are many kinds of flowers.
Flowers come in different shapes, sizes,
and colors. A flower can also be called
a **blossom**.

Flowers need water to grow. Most flowers get the water they need to grow from rain that falls from the sky.

Flowers also need sunlight to grow.
Some flowers need a lot of sunlight to
grow. Others need just a little sunlight
to grow.

seeds

Many flowers grow from **seeds** in the ground. Inside each seed is a tiny **root** and **stem**.

roots

Roots grow from the seed. The roots grow under the ground. They take in water and **minerals** that the plant needs to grow.

stem

A stem also grows from the seed. The stem carries water and minerals from the roots to the other parts of the plant.

leaves

Leaves grow from the stem. The leaves use **energy** from the sun to make food for the plant. The plant needs this food to live.

bud

A **bud** also grows from the stem. Some plants have small buds. Other plants have large buds.

A flower grows inside the bud. The outside of the bud protects the flower so it can grow. The bud will soon **bloom** and become a flower.

New seeds grow inside the flower. Inside
the seeds are tiny roots and stems of new
plants. These seeds will grow into new
plants and flowers.

Glossary

bloom   To open up.

blossom   A flower.

bud   A small, new, growing part on a plant.

energy   The power to live and grow.

leaves   The parts of a plant that make food for the plant.

minerals   Natural things that come from the soil and help plants grow.

root   The part of a plant that grows under the ground.

seeds   The parts of a plant that grow into new plants.

stem   The part of a plant that supports the plant. Leaves, buds, and flowers grow from the stem.